A Note to Parents and Caregivers:

Read-it! Readers are for children who are just starting on the amazing road to reading. These beautiful books support both the acquisition of reading skills and the love of books.

 The PURPLE LEVEL presents basic topics and objects using high frequency words and simple language patterns.

 The RED LEVEL presents familiar topics using common words and repeating sentence patterns.

 The BLUE LEVEL presents new ideas using a larger vocabulary and varied sentence structure.

 The YELLOW LEVEL presents more challenging ideas, a broad vocabulary, and wide variety in sentence structure.

 The GREEN LEVEL presents more complex ideas, an extended vocabulary range, and expanded language structures.

 The ORANGE LEVEL presents a wide range of ideas and concepts using challenging vocabulary and complex language structures.

When sharing a book with your child, read in short stretches, pausing often to talk about the pictures. Have your child turn the pages and point to the pictures and familiar words. And be sure to reread favorite stories or parts of stories.

There is no right or wrong way to share books with children. Find time to read with your child, and pass on the legacy of literacy.

Adria F. Klein, Ph.D.
Professor Emeritus
California State University
San Bernardino, California

Editor: Nick Healy
Designer: Abbey Fitzgerald
Page Production: Angela Kilmer
Art Director: Nathan Gassman
Associate Managing Editor: Christianne Jones
The illustrations in this book were created digitally.

Picture Window Books
5115 Excelsior Boulevard
Suite 232
Minneapolis, MN 55416
877-845-8392
www.picturewindowbooks.com

Printed in the United States of America.

Library of Congress Cataloging-in-Publication Data
Donahue, Jill L. (Jill Lynn), 1967-
Dad's shirt / by Jill L. Donahue ; illustrated by Jisun Lee.
p. cm. — (Read-it! readers)
Summary: When his father brings home a matching shirt for Cole, he is ecstatic,
but when something happens to the shirt, they need to find a creative solution.
ISBN-13: 978-1-4048-3163-6 (library binding)
ISBN-10: 1-4048-3163-0 (library binding)
ISBN-13: 978-1-4048-1228-4 (paperback)
ISBN-10: 1-4048-1228-8 (paperback)
[1. Fathers and sons—Fiction. 2. Problem solving—Fiction.] I. Lee, Jisun, 1978- ill.
II. Title.
PZ7.D714728Dad 2006
[E]—dc22   2006027284

Dad's Shirt

by Jill L. Donahue
illustrated by Jisun Lee

Special thanks to our advisers for their expertise:

Adria F. Klein, Ph.D.
Professor Emeritus, California State University
San Bernardino, California

Susan Kesselring, M.A.
Literacy Educator
Rosemount–Apple Valley–Eagan (Minnesota) School District

PiCTURE WiNDOW BOOKS
Minneapolis, Minnesota

Cole and his dad were best friends.
They loved to spend time together.

Cole wanted to be just like Dad.

One day, Dad came home with a special present for Cole.

The present was a shirt. It was yellow with black stripes.

Cole loved it! It was just like the one
Dad always wore.

Cole and Dad matched when they wore their shirts.

And they wore them everywhere.

They wore them when Cole helped
Dad work in the garden.

14

They wore them when they rode
their bikes.

They wore them when they went to the circus.

They wore them when they played with
Cole's train.

One day, Mom asked Cole and his dad to paint the fence.

They even wore their shirts while
they painted.

Cole had so much fun painting that he forgot about his shirt.

When he spilled paint on his hand,
he wiped it on his chest.

"Oh, no," said Dad. "Now our shirts don't match anymore."

Cole was sad. Then, he thought of a good plan.

He wiped his hand on Dad's shirt, too!

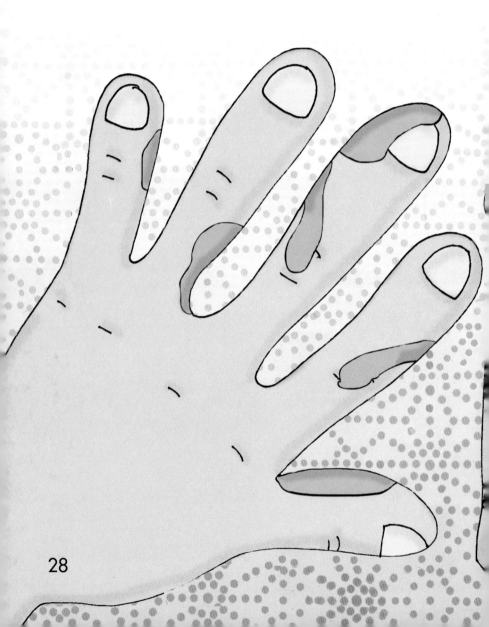

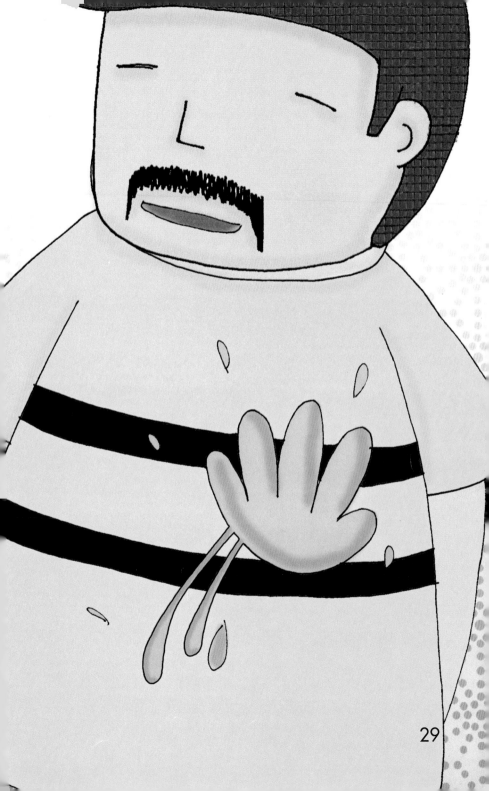

Cole laughed and yelled, "Now we match again, Dad!"

31

More *Read-it!* Readers

Bright pictures and fun stories help you practice your reading skills. Look for more books at your level.

Allie's Bike
The Bath
Busy Bear
Caleb's Race
Danny's Birthday
Days of the Week
Fable's Whistle
Finny Learns to Swim
Goldie's New Home
Jake Skates
New to Drew
The Princess and Her Pony
Riley Flies a Kite
The Tall, Tall Slide
The Traveling Shoes
Tricia's Talent
A Trip to the Zoo
Wendell the Worrier
Willy the Worm

Looking for a specific title or level? A complete list of *Read-it!* Readers is available on our Web site:
www.picturewindowbooks.com